MW00768954

3
FIG STREET KIDS
SERIES

Tommy's Race

Books by Sharon Hambrick

The Arby Jenkins Series
    Arby Jenkins
    Arby Jenkins, Mighty Mustang
    Arby Jenkins, Ready to Roll
    Stuart's Run to Faith
    Arby Jenkins Meets His Match
The Year of Abi Crim
Adoniram Judson: God's Man in Burma
The Fig Street Kids Series
    Tommy's Clubhouse
    Tommy's Rocket
    Tommy's Race

Tommy's Race

By Sharon Hambrick

Greenville, South Carolina

Library of Congress Cataloging-in-Publication Data
Hambrick, Sharon, 1961-
  Tommy's race / by Sharon Hambrick ; [illustrations by Maurie J. Manning].
      p. cm. — (The Fig Street kids)
  Summary: Over the summer, Tommy and the rest of the boys in his club make friends with William, who uses a wheelchair, compete in field day contests at the park, and enlist the whole town's support in raising money to buy a wheelchair for a poor boy in Kenya who has polio.
  ISBN 1-59166-286-9 (perfect bound pbk. : alk. paper)
  [1. Clubs—Fiction. 2. People with disabilities—Fiction. 3. Wheelchairs—Fiction. 4. Friendship—Fiction. 5. Moneymaking projects—Fiction.] I. Manning, Maurie, ill. II. Title.
  PZ7.H1755Tp 2004
  [Fic]—dc22

                                                  2004012060

Designed by Jon Kopp
Illustrations by Maurie J. Manning
Composition by Melissa Matos

© 2004 BJU Press
Greenville, SC 29614

Printed in the United States of America
All rights reserved

ISBN 1-59166-286-9

15 14 13 12 11 10 9 8 7 6 5 4 3 2 1

For Emma, Timmy,
Eddy, and Tommy

Contents

1
Birthday Money

On the last day of school, it was my birthday, but boy, was I upset! People were way more interested in getting out of school for the summer than they were in figuring out that I was eight years old. *Eight!*

Good thing I have a grandma who sends me money in a birthday card every year. That makes things a lot better than they would be if you didn't get a card, and everyone only said, "Have a nice summer." That's for sure.

Grandma always sends one dollar for how old you are, so I got eight dollars.

Penny looked at my card and the money that fell out. She said, "I got nine dollars for my birthday last month."

I said, "I know that, dummy," but Mom made me say sorry.

I'm not supposed to say *dummy* or *stupid* or other things like that that aren't super nice.

Mom said Happy Birthday and congratulations on being a third grader now. Penny said I wasn't a third grader until September when school started up again, but I said I was too a third grader right now because that's what you are when you finish second grade, which I did. I finished it! Just ask my teacher, Mr. Ramirez!

Penny said, "Too bad you only got eight dollars. You can't buy anything with eight dollars."

But I said I would too buy something superduper special with my eight dollars. Just wait and see.

Penny said too bad I would never be as old or smart as her, and I said I would catch up with her someday.

She said, "Nuh-uh."

It was going to start a fight, but Dad got home, so Mom brought out cake and ice cream. We lit candles, and everyone sang, "Happy Birthday, Dear Tommy."

And then I blew out my candles, easy-breezy, nothing to it. So I got to make a wish, which is this: to have a great great summer with my friends

Howie and Zack and Sammy. Those guys are my best friends for sure!

Here's some stuff about my friends.

First is Howie. Howie and I have been friends since before we ever went to school, because our moms used to take us in strollers down to Fig Street Park. We still go there all the time, but not in strollers. Now we ride our bikes. I can ride with one hand or with no hands, but only for a second, or I'll fall off.

Second is Zack. Zack lives across the street from Howie, and we have all been friends since he came to live here when we were in kindergarten. Zack can fly a Frisbee farther than anybody in

second grade, except now we are in third grade, so
we'll see if someone gets better than him.

Third is Sammy. Sammy lives on the corner
of Fig Street in a big house with his big brother
Nathan and his parents and his old grandpa who
is called Mr. Bolt. Mr. Bolt is the man who gave
me my dog Happy when I used to help him around
his house when he lived there alone. Sammy just
moved in part way through second grade, and
at first we weren't friends, but never mind that,
because now we are great friends!

I have other friends than these, but Howie and
Zack and Sammy are the main friends. We have
a great club called the Spy Guys. Mostly we sit
around my clubhouse and eat pretzels and talk
about going to the moon or finding buried treasure,
but sometimes we solve mysteries for people, or
we do jobs for money.

There are girls in our club too, but they have
their own day at the clubhouse, because there are
so many of us altogether that we can't stuff all of
us in the clubhouse at one time. So we have boys'
club time and girls' club time. I don't know what
the girls talk about, but probably it's not about
finding buried treasure. Once I tried to listen at the

door, but Penny came out and shouted at me to go home, so I did.

The girls in the club are Penny and Melodie and Elizabeth and Talia and Krissie and Megan. Maybe there are more, but I forget.

Never mind about the girls though. It's just Howie and Zack and Sammy that I was making the wish about having lots of fun with when I blew out my eight candles.

2
Summer Fun

On one of the first days of summer, Howie
and Zack and I were up in Sammy's bedroom. We
were playing a great game. It is called "Who can
make the craziest face?" We were sticking out our
tongues and making our eyes great big when all of
a sudden Sammy's mom called up the stairs.

"Sammy!" she said. "Come on down, Sweetie.
It's time to take out the trash!"

Sammy groaned, and the silly face he was
making slid right off!

"I hate taking out the trash," he said. "I hate it
worse than anything!"

We all agreed that taking out the trash was no
fun, especially if you have to do it when you would
rather be making faces with your friends.

"Sammy!" Mrs. Bolt called. "Do I have to
come up there and get you?"

"Quick, everyone," Sammy said. "Hide!"

He pushed us into the closet! We scrunched down as small as we could. Sammy started to whisper in the dark closet. "I'm sick of doing chores. I never want to do chores again."

We heard the bedroom door open. Mrs. Bolt said, "Sammy? I thought you were in here. Hmmm." The door closed, and we heard her footsteps going downstairs.

I was shaking! Because, for number one, it's not right to hide from your mom, even if it's your friend's mom, and for two, it's not right to not do your chores, because that's your part of being in the family. Plus, it's scary to hide with people in a dark closet. That's for sure.

Sammy said, "Okay, let's go."

"Go where?" I said.

"Just follow me."

I didn't know what else to do, so I did follow him. So did Howie and Zack. We snuck quiet as tiny mice down the hall. Sammy was in front so he could look out for his mom so we didn't run smack into her. We would be in trouble for that for sure!

"Sammy!" we heard. Mrs. Bolt was out in the backyard now. "Samuel Douglas Bolt, where are you?"

"Run," said Sammy. We tore down the stairs and ran out the front door and all the way to my house. We ran so fast we almost crashed into our neighbor Mrs. Mingo. She was walking all six of her dogs at once. I was glad we didn't fall over the dogs, because that would have slowed us down.

"Sorry, Mrs. Mingo," Howie said.

"Sorry, dogs!" shouted Zack.

"GO!" shouted Sammy, so we sped on to my house. We ducked behind the house and scrambled into my blue clubhouse as fast as we could! We were breathing hard.

"Good thing we got away," Sammy said. "When she starts yelling my whole name like that, I'm in a lot of trouble."

Happy, my dog, bounced into the clubhouse and jumped into my lap. I let her lick my face all over, and then I tickled her belly when she rolled over onto her back. She likes having her belly tickled.

"I know," I said. "One time I wanted to play slip-and-slide in the bathtub. I used pancake syrup instead of soap to make the tub slippery, and when my mom came in—oh boy, did she say my name out real loud. Like this—"

I stood up and shouted as loud as I could, "THOMAS ARTHUR JACKSON!"

I sat down. "It was like that," I said, but now I felt silly for shouting my name out so loud.

But Sammy didn't worry about that. He said. "I'm sick of taking out the trash."

"I'm sick of feeding the dog," Howie said.

"I'm sick of practicing piano," Zack said.

"I'm sick of loading the dishwasher!" I said.

Happy wasn't sick of anything. She kept wagging her tail as long as I scratched her tummy or behind her ears.

We talked about how it wasn't fair that we had to do chores, especially during summertime. We decided during vacation we should just play and play and solve a few mysteries so we would have money to buy ice cream on Main Street.

Then we talked about our usual clubhouse stuff, like going to the moon, and who is the fastest boy on Fig Street, and why girls are creepy, and if there's any buried treasure around here.

After a long time of talking we looked outside and saw that it was starting to get a little bit dark.

"The streetlights are on," I said. "It's time to go home." I stood up and Howie and Zack stood up.

"See you later," Howie and Zack said. Sammy didn't stand up.

"I already told you. I'm not going home for a million dollars," he said.

We all sat back down. "Oh," we said.

"The worst part of my life is doing chores," Sammy said, "I have to make my bed, and vacuum my room, and clean the upstairs bathroom, and take out the trash! I'm sick of it."

"Does Nathan do any chores?" I asked.

"He mows the lawn, and vacuums the house, and does the laundry," Sammy said.

"Plus, he's studying to be an astronaut," Howie said.

Nathan is Sammy's big brother. He's fifteen and is the smartest person I ever knew in my whole life. One time he helped me build a rocket that would really fly.

All of a sudden, a great idea popped into my head. "Hey," I said. "Let's move into the clubhouse! We can stay here all summer and never do any chores until school starts again."

The guys said, "Yeah!"

Happy thumped her tail.

Sammy said that was a really good idea. He said, "Good job, Tommy. You're the best," and that made me feel great.

"How are we going to tell our moms?" Howie asked.

"I won't tell anyone," Sammy said. "I'm staying here."

"My mom will cry," I said. "She likes having me home."

We decided that all the moms would cry, but we would give them tissues to blow their noses, and that would be nice of us. Howie said he might change his mind and keep living at home if his mom promised he didn't have to do any more chores all summer.

That seemed like a good idea, so we all agreed. If the moms said we had to still do chores, we would meet back at the clubhouse later tonight and never go home again. We said, "Spy Guys' honor" and shook hands on the deal.

"No more trash," said Sammy.

"No more practicing," Zack said.

"No more dog food," Howie said.

I said we still have to feed Happy because she is part of our club and doesn't know how to get her own food out of the bag.

Sammy stayed in the clubhouse with Happy while the rest of us went home to tell our moms we were moving out.

3
Moms on the Phone

It was already dinnertime, and the rest of the
family were already sitting in their places. I scooted
right up to the table and plunked down in my chair.
I had to wait to tell them about moving out because
Mom was reading a letter out loud to everyone.
The letter was from Uncle Mick. Uncle Mick is my
mom's brother, and he lives in Africa because he is
helping people build houses and learn to read.

The letter was like this:

Dear Melinda,

*Africa is an amazing place. It is such a large
place and so full of new experiences for me. I'm
really glad I could come and help out on these
projects.*

That's the sort of thing the letter was about,
telling about the houses he was building and the
kids he was teaching to read at the school. I was

so interested in the letter—because I love Uncle Mick a whole lot—that I forgot for a minute about moving out.

But later while we were eating, Mom said, "Okay, whose turn is it to load the dishwasher tonight?" and just like that, I remembered.

Penny said, "It's Tommy's turn."

But before I had a chance to say anything, the phone rang, and Mom said, "Excuse me," to go answer it.

Mom was gone a while on the phone, so I finished up all my dinner and thought about how to tell her the news. When she came back in a few minutes later, she had a funny look on her face. Sort of like a smile, but sort of not.

"Tommy, do you have something you want to tell us?" she said.

That surprised me. But since I did have something to say, I nodded.

"Yes, Son?" Dad said. "Go ahead."

"Well," I said, "the guys and me decided that we are sick of doing chores, so we are going to run away to the clubhouse for the whole summer."

Penny said, "What?" but Dad said "shhh" to her and turned back to look right at me.

"Really?" Dad said. "Is that the plan then?"

I said, "Yes, that is the plan." And then I remembered about the tissues, so I ran into the bathroom to get some for Mom, but there was no Kleenex, so I got a few squares of toilet paper. I ran back to the table and handed them to Mom.

Mom said, "What's this for?"

"It's for when you cry because I'm leaving," I said.

She just looked at me.

So I said, "But if you promise I don't have to do chores all summer, then I'll stay and you don't have to cry."

Penny said, "What?" again, but Dad looked at her in a funny way that was the same as saying, *be quiet for a minute, okay?*

That's when Mom started laughing. She only laughed a little bit, and then she put her hand over her mouth to stop the laughing from coming out. She didn't cry at all!

Instead she said, "Oh, by the way, that phone call was Rachel Oliver. She said Zack told her about the moving-out idea too. She'd already talked to Penny Mitchell and Susan Bolt, so I guess you boys are all in this together?"

"Yep, Spy Guys stick together," I said.

"Well, then," said Dad. He stood up, winked at Mom, and held out his hand to me for shaking. I shook his hand, but I didn't know why. Then he picked up my plate and cup from right in front of me.

"Hey," I said, "I'm not finished."

"Yes, actually, you are," Dad said, and he took my things right away from me.

When he came back in and sat down at the table again, I was still sitting there saying nothing. Penny was giving me dirty looks, but they weren't nearly as scary as some of the faces we had been making earlier up in Sammy's room, so I wasn't scared of her at all.

Dad said, "Are you still here? I thought you were moving out."

Penny started to laugh, but Dad gave her another look, and she got quiet.

"I'm going," I said. "But Mom's supposed to cry."

"Oh, no," said Mom. "All us moms agreed that boys who refuse to do chores have to live in the clubhouse all summer."

"You agreed?" I said.

"Yep," said Mom. "So I guess you'll be leaving now."

"I guess so," I said. I stuck out my tongue at Penny and said, "Ha, ha, you have to do all the chores now."

Mom walked over to the back door and opened it for me to go out.

I said, "Just a minute," and started to go upstairs to my room.

But Dad said, "Where are you going?"

"I'm going upstairs to get my things."

"What things are those?" Dad said.

"My pillow, my blanket, my clothes."

"Your mother and I paid for all of those things, Son," Dad said. "Those are our things. But we will allow you to take your toothbrush and the clothes you are wearing now."

"No pillow?" I said.

Mom and Dad shook their heads no, and Penny started to giggle. I got my toothbrush and slunk outside.

Mom didn't even kiss me goodbye.

4
All by Ourselves

"I only got to bring my toothbrush," said Howie.

"I got my toothbrush and today's *Fig Street Examiner*," Zack said.

"You brought the newspaper?" Howie said.

"Yeah," said Zack. "Mom said in case we got too cold out here, we could cover up with the pages."

"That sounds mean to me," I said, but then I noticed I hadn't been allowed to bring anything at all to cover up with, so the *Examiner* was maybe a great idea.

Sammy said, "Sleeping under the newspaper is better than doing chores."

I asked the guys if any of their moms had cried.

"Nope," they said. "Not one tear."

Even though it didn't start out with moms crying like we thought it would, we stayed up really late and had a lot of fun. We folded paper hats and boats out of the *Examiner*. We talked about being pirates and finding buried treasure and all the things we would do now that we didn't live at home anymore.

Penny knocked on the door when it was pitch-pitch black. "Here's a few blankets," she said. "And pillows. I didn't want you to be sad."

I said I wasn't sad, but then I started to think I was . . . just a teeny bit. I wanted my cozy bed, but I didn't say that to the guys, for sure!

In the morning it started to not be so fun anymore, because there was no breakfast. Also there was no bathroom and no toothpaste for our toothbrushes. I decided we could use the bathroom at my house, so we walked over there, and I went to open the door, but it was locked. I knocked.

My mom answered. "Yes?" she said, "May I help you?"

"We need the bathroom," I said.

"Hmm," said my mother. "I don't let strangers use my bathroom." She closed the door.

I started to cry, but stopped as soon as I could, because boys who move out of the house don't cry even if they are still kids.

"Let's try my house," Howie said, so we did, but his mom did the same thing. At Zack's house the same thing happened.

Sammy picked up a rock and threw it really hard at Zack's wooden fence. He stomped. He made some scary faces.

"The moms got together," he said. "We have to go home and say sorry, or we're never going to have any food or bathrooms again."

"We'll have to do chores," Howie said.

"Probably double chores for running away," Zack said.

"I'm in bad trouble," said Sammy.

But I said, "Moms don't play fair."

5
Spy Guys

After that we decided we would work on our Spy Guy business again. Sammy said if we solved enough mysteries, we would have enough money to pay our brothers and sisters to do our chores for us. Or maybe even have servants! That way we would get out of doing work and also become famous for solving big problems.

For the first few days, most of the mysteries we solved were like this: We would go to someone's house and knock on the door. We would ask if they had any problems that we could solve.

Mr. Bolt, Sammy's grandpa, said he had a big problem we could solve. He said he couldn't read the small print in the newspaper, and that was a huge problem.

I said, "We can't fix your eyes, Mr. Bolt."

He said, no, but we could read to him, so we took turns reading in the *Fig Street Examiner* about the San Diego Padres and the New York Yankees. Then we decided to start lifting weights and running fast races so we could be baseball players when we grew up. Mr. Bolt told us to study, study, study because education is how you get ahead in life, and never mind the baseball unless it's just for fun.

Howie said Mr. Bolt is just jealous because he's not a baseball player. But I said to leave Mr. Bolt alone, because he is always nice to us, and he gave me my dog Happy.

Some people had problems like too many weeds in their yard or ants in their kitchen. Mrs. Mingo said, "Yes, yes, come right in. The dogs need a bath, and I'm completely piled up with housework." She showed us the dogs and the hose and the dog shampoo in her backyard and said, "Have a lot of fun, boys."

When I wash Happy, it's no problem, because she's a small dog, and she's my friend. But Mrs. Mingo's dogs were superbig and hairy! We argued about whether to wash all of them at once or one at a time. Pretty soon we lined up all the dogs up in a line, like a car wash.

We had to get them wet and then soapy and
then rub the soap in real good to get all the way
down to the skin, and then we had to rinse them off
real good.

It was hard work, but fun because at the end
the dogs were shaking themselves off, and Sammy
was spraying all of us with the hose, and we ended
up wetter than the dogs.

Mrs. Mingo came out and gave us each a dollar.
She said it looked like we did a great job, and she
hoped we weren't in any trouble for being so wet.

We took our dollars to Andy's Candies on Main
Street. We were dripping wet, but, oh well. We
bought boxes of red licorice and some Whoppers.

Whoppers are malted milk balls, and they come in a box that looks like a milk carton.

When we got back to the clubhouse, we played a game called "How much candy can you put in your mouth at once." It is a really gross thing to do, especially if you fold up the licorice and stuff it in, and then put in a few Whoppers. We had huge pouchy cheeks full of candy when there was a knock on the door.

I opened the door, and there was Mrs. Peeples! Mrs. Peeples is the oldest person on our street. She has sparkly eyes behind her glasses and little white curls all over her head.

My mouth was crazy full of chewy red licorice and chocolate brown balls! When I opened my mouth to say "Hello"—because you have to say hello—lots of candy just fell out. I turned around to see what the other guys were doing, and they were spitting and pulling candy out of their mouths.

It was gross! All over the floor of the clubhouse were licorice sticks and half-chewed chocolate balls all covered with spit.

We wiped our mouths with our hands and looked at Mrs. Peeples. She laughed right at us! Mrs. Peeples is almost ninety years old, so

I thought she would think we were the most disgusting things she had ever seen.

"You boys," she said. "You are so funny!" We were all ashamed, but Mrs. Peeples said, "Back in the thirties, when I was in college, I once swallowed five goldfish." She winked at us.

"Oh," we said, and then we had nothing to do except pretend the floor wasn't covered in drooly candy and see what Mrs. Peeples wanted.

"I have a little mystery for you boys," she said. "There's a nice crisp dollar bill for each one of you if you solve it."

We smiled and said, "Okay."

"My granddaughter-in-law has come to live with me for the summer," Mrs. Peeples said. "Her husband (my grandson) is in the Navy, and he is away on a ship for a while, so she brought herself and her son William to stay with me for a while, isn't that nice?"

"Yes," we nodded. That seemed nice.

"Well, boys, the mystery is this: Where is William going to get some good friends to play with over the summer? Who will play with him? Who will invite him over? Who might have a club he could join?"

"Me, me!" I said. "I have a club!"

But Sammy said, "How come you have to pay people to be his friends?"

"Rude!" said Howie.

But Zack said, "Yeah, how come?"

Mrs. Peeples looked down at the ground and seemed sad.

I thought, oh, no what if she starts crying, because I don't have any Kleenex or toilet paper squares for her, and what if she cries herself to death?

Then she smiled. "Well, you are smart boys," she said, looking at Sammy. "You figured out there must be something different about William that makes it a little bit harder for him to make friends."

Sammy smiled around at all of us. "See?" he said, "I am supersmart."

"William can't walk," Mrs. Peeples said. "Sometimes this makes people nervous to be around him and afraid to be his friend."

"We'll be his friends," I said. "We're not afraid."

"You don't even have to pay us!" Howie said.

I thought I wanted to get the money.

But Zack said, "Not even a penny!" So there went our money!

"Good," said Mrs. Peeples. She smiled and her face got even crinklier than ever.

"We'll be best friends with him," I said. "He can be a Spy Guy!"

Mrs. Peeples's face crinkled right up into a smile. "Good," she said. "Why don't you come and meet him tomorrow morning." We said we would do that, and then she said, "Do you have any more licorice?"

I looked at the floor where are the slimy, spitty licorice was.

"Not that kind," she said. Sammy laughed and gave her a brand new piece from his box. She said thank you and went home chewing on it.

The next morning we met at my house. We decided we were nervous after all, so Mom said she would go with us.

I said, "I never met anybody before with no legs."

"Who said William doesn't have any legs?" Mom said.

"Well," I said, "Mrs. Peeples said William can't walk. That means he doesn't have any legs. If he had legs, he could walk."

Mom said maybe he had legs and maybe he didn't, but that didn't make any difference, because the important thing to remember was to be nice to William and make sure we were really great friends with him.

Mom got a peach pie out of the oven and said she was ready to go see William's mom to welcome her to the neighborhood. We all tromped down there to meet William and even Happy went with us, but she would run ahead and then run back and then run around in circles after her tail.

Mom and Mrs. Peeples and William's mom went off to the kitchen to have tea and talk about everything like ladies always do.

We boys said hello to William and looked to see if he had legs. He did, but they didn't work, so he sat in a wheelchair. "Come on out back," he said. "Wanna see what I can do with my chair?"

We said yeah and followed him out back.

It turned out he could push himself forward or backward, or even in circles! After that we went back to his bedroom, which used to be Mrs. Peeples's sewing room. It still looked like a sewing room, because it had flowery wallpaper, and it smelled like Mrs. Peeples. But it had something that made it better than anything. Around the whole room, William had put a train set!

It has engines and cabooses and all the other little cars, plus fake trees and little tiny railroad stations. He has to get out of his chair to play trains, and since he can't walk, he scoots himself around the room, which is kind of creepy. No wonder he doesn't have friends. But we decided we would still be his friends, because we promised Mrs. Peeples, and she is one of our favorite people.

"We meet in the clubhouse every day if you want to be a Spy Guy," I said to William.

"Okay," he said. "I'll come."

"Too bad we don't have a train set like this in the clubhouse," said Howie.

We all agreed that would be great, but too bad we don't have any money to buy one.

"Too bad," we all said.

"We could meet here sometimes," William said. "We could have club in my room maybe." He looked around at us. I had a frown on my face for sure, because club is supposed to happen in a clubhouse, and that means my blue clubhouse because it's the best place in the whole world for having a club. That's what I say.

"Great idea, William," said Sammy, "especially if we get to do the train. I love trains. They're not as great as rockets, but they are really great."

I wasn't happy about having club in William's room, but I said, "Okay, but only once in a while."

"How about now?" said William, so we all sat down on the floor and played trains. It was really great and young Mrs. Peeples brought us lemon cookies and smiled down on us.

When we left, old Mrs. Peeples said we were great friends. She tried to give us dollars, but we didn't take them, because we liked William, and we wanted to be his friends and play with his train set.

Pretty soon everyone wanted to have club at William's house all the time.

"It's better than the clubhouse," Howie said, "because there's lemon cookies and trains."

6
The Letter

Things got even worse after that, because now that Spy Guys were meeting at William's room every day, the Spy Girls club could meet all the time in the blue clubhouse. My clubhouse full of girls! Yuck!

Pretty soon they put in plants and dolls and boxes of stickers and pretty paper for writing letters. Who writes letters in a clubhouse? That's what I wanted to know. All that stuff in there made me mad!

"Hey," I said to the girls. "This is my clubhouse. Mine! Mine!"

"So sit down," said Melodie. "We're trying to think of a good deed we can do this summer to be good citizens. My mother says we have to contribute to our community even though we are only little kids."

"I don't want to do good deeds," I said. "I want my clubhouse back."

I sat there with the girls for a while. They were deciding about sending toys to Maria, the girl they support in Guatemala. I thought about the Spy Guys who were right this minute playing trains in William's room at Mrs. Peeples's house. They were probably eating lemon cookies or maybe even chocolate chip cookies today. I was mad about everything, and just then there was a knock on the door. I didn't answer it because Penny jumped up and got there before me. It was Mom outside.

"Is Tommy in here?" she said.

"Yes, I'm here," I said. I was moping.

"Mail came," she said. "A letter for you from Uncle Mick."

I jumped right up and shouted, "Yes!"

Uncle Mick is the best uncle in the world. He is loud and happy, and he takes me out for ice cream. Not right now he doesn't, because he's in Africa helping people, but when he comes home, then we will eat lots and lots of ice cream, and that's the best thing in the world for sure!

"What's in the letter?" Penny said.

I decided I was not going to read Uncle Mick's letter in front of all the girls, so I said, "It's guy stuff," and I went outside. But all of a sudden here came Howie and Zack and Sammy and William to find me.

So what happened was we all crammed into the clubhouse, and I said, "Look, I got this letter from Africa, from Uncle Mick."

And everyone said, "Read it!"

So I read it, and that is how the Spy Guys and the Spy Girls learned about Joseph in Nairobi and how he is learning to read and how he has to sit in a chair all the time because his legs don't work at all!

"Why doesn't he use a wheelchair like William?" Zack said.

And a lot of other people said, "Yeah."

And William said, "Yeah. Find out why he doesn't just use a wheelchair like me. I'm a super-duper wheeler man. Zooming around the whole clubhouse."

The clubhouse isn't that big, so he didn't get to wheel around much, plus the girls were saying, "Stop it, William!"

Except for Melodie. She was sitting there thinking, and then she said, "I think we should write a letter to Uncle Mick and find out about Joseph. That's what I think."

"Yeah," everyone said.

But I said, "No, I'm not going to write a letter during summer, because writing letters is like school. And I don't want to think about school during the summer."

But William said we had to because if he didn't have a wheelchair he would want other kids to wonder why.

Melodie passed everyone a piece of pretty writing paper. She said to remember about the return address and salutation and body and closing and signature—all the stuff that's in letters. But I sat in the corner and wrote my letter without any of that, just with *Dear Uncle Mick* and then my letter and then *Love, Tommy.* That's it!

We had a big fight over who got to mail the letters. The fight got so big, Penny said, "Let's let Mom decide." So we went into the house—all of us!—and told Mom about the problem.

"There's ten of us, and we all want to mail the letters!"

Mom looked at us for a few minutes, and then she said, "Sit down." We all sat down. That's when she told us the bad news. It takes forever for a letter to get to Africa, maybe more than a month! At that speed, it would be two whole months before we got a letter back. I stood up. I said, "I want to know about Joseph now."

Mom said, "I have a great idea. Come on upstairs, everyone!"

We all trooped up the stairs in a long line, and Mom got into her e-mail program. She let each of us type one sentence in a letter to Uncle Mick. Then she wrote a few things at the bottom of the letter and pushed *send*.

"There!" she said. "That'll be in Kenya today."

I said, "I love computers, and that is for sure!"

I said, "He'll write back today!"

Mom said maybe he would, but don't count on it because Uncle Mick is very, very busy, and he isn't always in the office to get mail. "Maybe he is out in a village building houses. He'll get the letter when he gets it. Then he'll write back."

I didn't want to wait at all!

7
Big Announcement

At breakfast, Dad said, "Hey, look at this!" while he was reading the *Fig Street Examiner*. "The park is going to have a field day for all the kids."

"Yea!" said Penny.

And Mom said, "That sounds fun."

But I said, "What's field day?"

Dad said it was a day full of races and games and food.

"And prizes!" said Penny.

"Prizes!" I said. I hopped out of my seat and ran around the dining room. "I want to win!" I said. "I want to win, win, win!"

Mom said, "Thomas, sit down," but at least she didn't said *Thomas Arthur Jackson*, so I wasn't in trouble.

I wanted it to be my turn to win something. Sammy and Melodie always won the spelling bees, and Howie always won the running races. Zack was great at jumping out of swings the farthest, and now William was everybody's favorite because of his train set and even having club in his room instead of my clubhouse where it belonged.

I said, "I hate that William."

But then Mom said, "Thomas Arthur Jackson," and I had to say sorry and then explain how that came up since we were talking about the field day.

"Oh yeah. Field Day." I said. "I forgot. I'm going to win!"

Dad read us the article in the paper. All kids up to eighteen years old could play, but don't worry because the big teenagers won't be in the same race with eight-year-olds. It depends on how old you are what race you are in. Also if you were a grownup, you could sign up to be in charge of a game or race or bringing pies to sell. Mom said she would make pies and also run a game.

"What kind of game?" Penny said. "Can I help you, Mom?"

Mom decided she would make one of those games where you throw the beanbag through the wooden clown's open mouth, and we could give out little prizes like yo-yos or whistles.

Dad said the city was going to pay for the ribbons for the athletic contests and trophies for the big kids' races. He said, "A white ribbon is for third place, a red ribbon is for coming in second, and a blue ribbon is for being first."

"I want blue!" I said.

Penny said, "Shhh, let Dad read!"

But I said, "I like blue."

When I got to William's house that morning for club meeting, the guys were already talking about the field day. We wanted to go right down to the park to sign up. When we got there, there was Mrs. Mingo at a table with all her dogs sitting there real polite. She said we could sign up for three contests. There was fifty-yard dash, Frisbee throw, long jump, high jump, kickball, shoot baskets, and jumping rope. She said some high school boys would be helping at the park over the next few weeks to make sure we learned the skills for how to do the race or contest. "It will make it more fair," she said. "If everyone has a little training."

I said I didn't need any training, but Howie and Zack said to be quiet and just sign up.

"Write your name by the three things you want to do at field day," Mrs. Mingo said, "so I can make lists for the high school boys of who needs to learn what skill."

I wanted to run and run, so I signed up for the fifty-yard dash. After that I decided to kick the kickball, and throw a Frisbee, because those are things I already know how to do, so if I don't learn very well in practice time, I would still be okay and maybe even win.

Before we walked home, I saw that William had signed up for fifty-yard dash too. I looked over at him sitting in his wheelchair under a tree talking to Howie and Sammy, and I thought he must have made a mistake. He must have signed up for the fifty-yard dash by accident, when what he really wanted to do was throw the Frisbee.

I ran right over to the tree. I said, "William, you made a mistake. You signed up for fifty-yard dash instead of Frisbee. Want me to fix it for you?"

William said, "No mistake, Tommy. I'm going to do the dash. I'm going to dash and dash and dash!"

I looked down at his legs and said, "Did your legs get fixed or what?"

He said, "Nope. I'm going to push myself in my chair like always."

So I said, "That's crazy. You'll be last. You'll be so far behind, it'll be crazy!"

"I'm going to try to win," William said.

I said, "You'll never win."

That's when William got kind of sad. He said, "I know I can't win, but I want to try."

"Why try if you can't win?" I said.

And William said, "I want to hear people yelling, *Go, William!*"

I thought the other guys would say that William was nuts too, but they didn't.

Howie said, "Good for him."

And Zack said, "It doesn't hurt to try."

And Sammy said, "Wouldn't it be great if William did win?"

But what I thought was, *I want to be in that race, because at least I won't be in last place. Maybe I can win a blue ribbon!*

8
Joseph

For two weeks we hung around the park
practicing our skills with the high school boys. I
changed from kicking the ball to jumping rope,
because I found out I could go a lot of times with
the jump rope without missing, and that's what that
contest is all about—who can go the longest.

Some kids said jumping rope was just for girls,
so I asked Mrs. Mingo, and she said anyone could
do it. So I said, "See?" and kept my name for jump
rope. I can jump over a hundred times, I bet!

I kept checking to see if William was going
to change from the fifty-yard dash, but he never
did. He also signed up for Frisbee throw. I
watched him, and I learned something. William
is supergreat at Frisbee throw. It doesn't take any
legs at all to throw a Frisbee, but you have to have
strong arms.

I told Mrs. Mingo at the park. I walked right up to her and said, "It's not fair for William to do Frisbee throw."

Mrs. Mingo stopped scratching between her dog's ears. She said, "Why's that Tommy?"

I said, "Because William has stronger arms than the rest of us because of wheeling himself around all the time."

Mrs. Mingo said it was plenty fair and that I should not worry about it. She said everyone gets to sign up for whatever three skills they want, and it doesn't matter if someone is strong or not strong.

Then one day Melodie ran right up into William's room. She said, "Guys! Come to the clubhouse! Tommy's mom finally got an e-mail from Uncle Mick!"

We plopped William right into his wheelchair and zoomed fast over to my house so we could hear Mom read the letter. I wanted to know the answer to why Joseph sits around all day and doesn't just use his wheelchair.

It took a long time for everyone to be quiet for the letter, but finally Sammy said, "Be quiet or else!"

So we all got superquiet so Mom could read. This is the letter.

Dear Fig Street Kids,

Thanks for your great e-mail! Sorry it took me so long to reply. I have been out building houses and teaching English all the time. By the end of the day, I'm tired!

I read your letter to Joseph! He was happy to hear from kids in America. I showed him America on the world map, and I even pointed out where Fig Street is. If you go to the library, you can find Kenya on the big globe. If you look really closely, maybe you can see Nairobi. That's the city where we live. We are on the eastern coast of Africa, next to the Indian Ocean.

Here are the answers to all your questions. Joseph is eight years old. He used to be able to walk, but he got a disease called polio, and now his legs don't work any more. Sometimes he uses crutches to get around. He doesn't have a wheelchair because his family is very poor, and there is no money to buy him one.

Keep writing to me. Joseph says hello and now that he knows how to write his name, he will type his name below mine.

Love,

Uncle Mick

Joseph

Right away Melodie said, "That's not right. Everyone who needs a wheelchair should have a wheelchair. How come they don't buy him one even if they are poor? Lots of poor people have wheelchairs."

Mom said things are different in Africa. Lots of people are superpoor and don't even have dinner every day.

Zack said, "No way!"

But Howie said "is so" because he saw it on National Geographic on television.

Melodie said we have to go to the library right now to find out if everyone in Africa is poor and how come nobody fixes that? And also to look at the big globe and see where Kenya is because nobody knows.

Elizabeth said, "I don't even know where Africa is, or even America." But she said it really quietly so only I could hear, and I said I would show her. But I'm not really sure either.

By the time we got to the library, we were shouting "Wheelchair for Joseph!" We only stopped when we got to the library because of two things. The first thing was there was a man sitting outside, and he looked sort of scary, and the second thing is you're supposed to be quiet at the library so people can read and not be bothered by you. And if you do talk, everyone says, "Shhh!" and that makes you ashamed of yourself.

Melodie walked straight up to Miss Brenda because she is the boss of the whole library. Miss Brenda said, "Hello, Melodie. Hello, all of you. What can I do for you today?"

Miss Brenda is everyone's friend because she has been checking out books for us since we were very small and only had books with one word on a page like "shoe" and "sock" and "baby." Now we read big books like *The Cat in the Hat*, but Melodie's mom won't let her read *The Cat in the Hat* because she says, "Why does that mother leave her children alone all day while she goes to town?"

I said, "Oh" to that because I don't know why the mother leaves, but it seems like a lot of fun to have the Cat in the Hat come around. And I hope my mom leaves me alone sometime with Penny, so the Cat can come to our house and let out Thing 1 and Thing 2. As long as they clean up. Because if they don't clean up before they leave, I will be in a superlot of trouble, and Mom will say *Thomas Arthur Jackson* again, and that means trouble, trouble, trouble!

Miss Brenda said, "What can I do for you today?"

Melodie said, "Why is Africa sick and poor? How come Joseph doesn't have a wheelchair? What is polio? Can I get polio? Where is Kenya? Where is Nairobi? Does everyone in Africa have brown skin?"

She asked so many questions Miss Brenda put up her hands and said, "Slow down, Melodie! You're knocking me over!" And then she pretended to fall over into her chair, but really she just sat down, so she didn't get hurt.

Miss Brenda made us all come over to the reading corner and sit down. Then she said, "Okay, what is this about?" So we showed her Uncle Mick's letter. She read it and then said, "My, my. We do have a problem, don't we?"

"Yes, we do," said Melodie. "We need to know why is everyone sick and poor in Africa, and where is Kenya, and what is polio—"

"STOP!" said Miss Brenda, but she was smiling. "Let's look at the globe."

She walked us over to the globe and showed us where we live in America and then how you have to travel across the country to the Atlantic Ocean. And then you have to get on a boat and sail across

the whole ocean, and there is Africa. And then you have to get out your jungle knife and hack and hack and hack through all the jungles from one side of Africa to the other, and there is Kenya. And the capital city of Kenya is called Nairobi, and that's where Uncle Mick and Joseph live.

I said, "I would take an airplane instead of a jungle knife."

"Well, yes," Miss Brenda said, "That would be much much easier."

"Plus no tigers that way," said Elizabeth.

I don't like tigers except if they are in a cage at the zoo or stuffed like the tiger I have from my fifth birthday, even though one ear is torn off and his neck had to be sewn up by Mom when it tore.

Miss Brenda wouldn't tell us all the answers to our questions. She said, "Let's get you all checked out with some great books so you can find the answers to your questions."

Melodie said, "Why don't you just tell us the answers?"

And Miss Brenda said, "I don't know everything, do I?"

I said, "Yes, you do."

And she said, "Well, maybe I do, but you still need to practice your figure-it-out and learn-it-yourself skills so you can be a success in your life."

I said, "I just want to know the answers."

But she packed us out the door with piles of books about Africa and kids who had polio and kids who need wheelchairs.

Guess what I learned? There was a president of the United States who had polio, and he couldn't walk at all! It wasn't Abraham Lincoln, so don't worry about that. It was Franklin Roosevelt, and he had to use a wheelchair or he couldn't go anywhere!

Melodie said that was the greatest thing she ever heard, and she wanted to write to Joseph right now that somebody with polio was president and so maybe he could be president someday too. "You never know," she said.

We saw the scary man again outside the library. Elizabeth said hello to him, and he said hello back, and Elizabeth ran away fast.

I said, "Why did you run?"

And she said the man scared her because he looks all scruffy and dirty and like he wants to eat up little girls.

I said, "Why did you say hello to him then?"

And she said she was saying hello to a bluebird, but the man made a mistake and thought she spoke to him.

Elizabeth hiccupped the whole afternoon because that's what happens to her when she gets scared.

Melodie said to stop it, that the man has been sitting there for a long time, and he doesn't bother anyone. It's just that he doesn't have anywhere to go, so he might as well sit at the library. And we should just keep our eyes open and not get into cars with strangers or take candy unless the person is our parents or Mrs. Peeples or Mrs. Mingo or someone like that.

After the library we went to the park so we could get help with our skills from the high school boys. Nathan Bolt and some of his friends were there, and they were going to help us. Today we were going to study how to jump rope.

I got mad right off because some of the girls can jump a zillion times in a row, and they can cross the jump rope in front of them or even jump two girls in one jump rope.

I said, "It's not fair that the girls can sign up for jump rope, because they are better at it than the boys!"

Mrs. Mingo said, "Never mind about that. Anyone can sign up for whatever they want."

Some girl I don't even know came up to me and said, "Too bad we're better than you. You'll never win jump rope."

So that got me mad, and I said, "I can jump rope way better than you!"

That made me decide that I would be the best jumper in the whole world. I sure wasn't going to let those girls beat me. No way!

So I got a jump rope from Mrs. Mingo, and I went over with Nathan and a few other boys, and I started to jump. I jumped and jumped and jumped. Then I jumped some more! I said if a girl can jump three hundred times a boy can jump three million times without missing. That's what I think about boys being better than girls at jump rope.

While I was jumping an idea came to me. I was thinking and jumping so much I forgot to count how many. But pretty soon the great idea stopped my thinking about my jumping, and I tripped over the rope.

Who cares! I threw the rope on the ground and ran over to the girls who were practicing with some high school girls. I said, "Hey! I have a great idea!"

So Melodie said, "Wait a minute." And then she jumped for another hundred jumps.

"Stop," I said. "I have a great idea!"

So Melodie stopped, and all the kids gathered around me and said, "What?"

And I said, "Us Fig Street Kids could raise money and buy Joseph a wheelchair."

At first no one said anything, but then everyone started saying, "Yeah!" and "Great idea!" and "I have three dollars in dimes" and other stuff like that.

As soon as we finished practicing our jumping, we ran back to the clubhouse to talk about it some more.

"It's perfect," Melodie said. "This is just the thing we need to do to be good citizens."

And William wheeled over to me and said, "Cool idea, Tommy." And I felt supergreat about that!

9
Four Hundred Seventy-six

Mom and Dad and even my sister Penny thought that my idea about getting a wheelchair for Joseph was supergreat. We talked about it all through dinner, but sometimes I had to stop talking so I could chew my food. I'm not allowed to swallow my food without chewing it ten times for each mouthful. Except with ice cream. That's different. You can't chew ice cream at all. It will make your teeth hurt, so you just swallow it.

Dad said, "Getting a wheelchair for Joseph is a great aspiration, son."

I said, "What is *aspiration*?"

And Dad said, "It means hope."

So I said, "Then why'd you say aspiration, if you meant hope?"

Dad said never mind about that, but that the first thing we needed to do was get online and see what a wheelchair costs, and then how much it costs to send it to Kenya.

I wanted to do that right away. Getting online means using the computer, and I hardly ever get to do that! Mom said we had to wait until after dessert because Penny had made something extra special in her cooking class.

I said, "What, what?" because I always want to know what's coming, especially if it's dessert!

Penny said, "It is my famous chocolate pie." She was smiling, so I know she was very happy that she had made a chocolate pie. I was very happy too. I love chocolate, and I love pie, so I knew I would love chocolate pie supermuch.

The pie was great, and I said, "mmm, great," so many times, that I forgot about getting online.

Then Dad said, "Okay, Tommy, after you finish your chores, come on upstairs and we'll look for wheelchair prices."

I jumped up and said, "Yes!" But I knocked over my plate of pie, and it fell *boom* onto the floor! That meant I had extra cleaning-the-floor chores before my regular chores. By the time I was ready to look at the computer with Dad, I was about to pop from excitement.

Dad searched for "wheelchairs" which I wanted to do, because I know how to search and point and click and right-click and double-click and everything. Dad says it's funny that someone who is barely eight years old knows more about computers than some grown people. I felt smart when he said that.

"It'll cost about twenty dollars, I bet!" I said, because twenty dollars is more than I could ever afford.

Dad said, "Oh, it'll be much more than that."

But I said, "No way!"

Way! It was much more than twenty dollars. We found a place that sells them for two hundred and forty-seven dollars.

"Who has two hundred and forty-seven dollars?" I shouted.

Then there was even worse news. Dad said, "We'll have to find out how much it costs to ship the wheelchair to Kenya."

Penny came to up to see why I was shouting.

"Why are you shouting?" she said.

So I said, "Because it costs two hundred and forty-seven dollars to buy a wheelchair!"

And then Dad said, "Let's see. The United States Postal Service charges two hundred twenty-

one dollars and fifty cents. Plus, we'll want to insure it to make sure it gets there safely. That's another six dollars. Plus a return receipt, that's a buck seventy-five, for a grand total of two hundred twenty-nine dollars and twenty-five cents!"

I stopped shouting. I fell on the floor and cried instead. Penny started to cry too, because even she knows two hundred and forty-seven plus two hundred and twenty-nine is like a million zillion dollars, and we could never get that much in all the rest of our lives!

Penny said, "Stop crying, and I will give you my nine dollars from my birthday."

"You will?" I said.

She nodded. "Joseph needs it," she said.

"Wow," I said. "Neat." But I was still crying a teeny tiny bit, but not enough for anyone to notice. Then I did the problem on a piece of paper. It added up to four hundred seventy-six dollars and twenty-five cents.

Penny said, "Let's say four seventy-six, that's easier."

I said okay, but it was definitely not okay.

Mom came in and hugged us all. She said we should both get onto her lap, and she would tell us a little story. Me and Penny snuggled up on Mom even though we're not little babies anymore. Mom's lap was crowded. She told us the little story.

"When your Grandpa Plummer was a little boy, he got a disease called polio. Lots of kids used to get polio in the old days."

I said, "That's what Joseph had!"

Mom nodded and said to hush while she told the story. I hushed right up!

"Grandpa's family was very poor, and they didn't have enough money to get him to the doctor," Mom said. "But then all the kids in the family started to do extra jobs around the neighborhood. Pretty soon the neighbors and the storeowners wanted to know why the Plummer kids were working so hard, and pretty soon everyone knew it was so Grandpa could go to the doctor.

"When they found that out, everyone started to bring pennies to the house and drop them off on the step. Pretty soon, there were enough pennies to take the sick little boy to the doctor."

"And he got all better!" I shouted.

But Penny said, "Shhh."

And Mom said, "Listen."

It turned out he did not get better at all.

"In fact," Mom said, "the doctor said his legs wouldn't work again, and he would need crutches to get around."

"Was there money to buy crutches?" Penny asked.

Mom said, "No, there wasn't any more money."

"Well, what did they do?" I said. "Did they make him sit in a chair like Joseph and never go anywhere ever again, ever?"

And Mom said, "Nope. They started to do more jobs. They worked harder and harder, and after a long time, they had enough money to buy crutches. Everyone helped and the job got done."

"I will do jobs for Joseph," I said.

"Me, too," said Penny.

For club the next day, Penny made sure all the girls came, so it was all the girls and all the boys squashed into the clubhouse. It was squishy. I told about what Dad found out about how much it costs to buy a wheelchair and mail it to Africa.

Elizabeth started to hiccup when I said the part about almost five hundred dollars.

Then Penny stood up and told Mom's story about kids doing chores to help out.

We started to talk about how many jobs it would take and how long we would have to work. Then someone knocked on the door. It was Nathan Bolt. He was coming to get Sammy for lunch, but Sammy said, "Come in and help us, Nathan."

So we told him the whole story about Joseph and the four hundred seventy-six dollars and how it was totally impossible!

Nathan got a piece of paper out of his pocket and a pen. He wrote:

We need $476 for Joseph's wheelchair.

He held it up for us to see. Then he sat down on the table, looked around and said, "Does anyone have this much?"

No one did. Then he said, "Does anyone have any ideas for getting this much?"

I said, "We can do jobs around town!"

So Nathan wrote *jobs* on the paper.

Melodie said, "We should have a penny drive." It turns out that having a penny drive means you go around and ask people for pennies. "Everyone has pennies to give away," Melodie said.

So we decided to do both things. We would all try to do extra jobs when we could, and also we would ask people for their extra pennies.

Then Nathan had to go and make it super-horrible by asking us to figure out how many jobs we would need to do. "How many jobs?" he said. "How many pennies?"

We decided we could get about fifty cents for a job. William figured out that it would take more than nine hundred jobs to get four hundred and seventy-six dollars.

I said, "No way!"

That worked out to about a hundred jobs apiece and that's not counting if you take some of the money to buy candy because you're so hungry after working so hard.

When Nathan wrote about so many jobs each, I said, "That's crazy. We can never do that!"

Some of the kids said, "Yeah, it's crazy."

Nathan said, "Fine. Forget all about it. Joseph can sit on the bench and never wheel around. Who cares?"

There was silence in the clubhouse for a minute until William said, "I care."

Then people said "I care too" and "We can do it" and "Don't give up before we even start" and stuff like that.

So Nathan said, "Okay, Fig Street Kids, what do you say? Do we try to earn the money or do we give up right now?"

"We try," said Sammy.

"We definitely try," said Penny.

We took a vote and everyone voted for trying. I voted for trying even though I think it's crazy, because it's not fun if everyone else raises their hands for something and you don't. Then people might look at you and call you names.

After the vote, everyone started saying "Okay!" and "Yeah!" And so that's how we started *Jobs and Pennies for Joseph*.

Our motto was, "Nothing is impossible."

10
More Chores Than Ever

"It's ridiculous that we are doing extra chores," Howie said. "We are the guys who never wanted to do chores again."

We all agreed it was crazy, but that we wanted to do the chores because we wanted to earn the money for the new wheelchair. We picked weeds. We washed dogs. We folded laundry. We took Zack's red wagon around the street and collected books that needed to go back to the library. We did anything we could think of that people would give us a little money for.

Mom and Dad said I was working so well that they were going to start paying me a little bit for my chores.

"Wow," I said. "That's great!"

Penny asked if she could get paid for her chores too if she promised to give some to the Joseph project. That's how me and Penny started getting paid a little bit for doing our regular chores. But only if we did them really great, because if you only pretend to do the chore, like if you leave half the dishes in the sink, you don't get paid. Then you have to go to bed early, and you have to say sorry.

Nathan pitched in too. He went around the street and offered to help kids with their math facts so they wouldn't forget them over the summer if the parents would pay him a dollar. None of the kids wanted to come to his class, but the parents wanted them to, plus they thought it was nice he was giving money to the Joseph Project, so they made us all go.

Aside from jobs, we also walked up and down Fig Street every day with our jars and asked people if they had any more pennies. After a couple of days people would have their pennies ready for us.

We even went over to Main Street and stopped at the businesses. Almost everyone gave us something, and some of the businesses let us put jars out to collect even more pennies. But there was one place that wouldn't help. It was called Nettleman's Medical Supply. Nettleman's wouldn't give us anything.

I said, "Hello, Mr. Nettleman, would you like to give us some pennies? We are saving up pennies to buy a wheelchair for a boy in Africa."

Mr. Nettleman said, "Now, young man, I wouldn't have a successful business, would I, if I gave all my profits away?"

I said, "I don't know."

But he looked right at us and said, "I take in money here, boys. I don't give it out."

He scared me, and I got out of there fast. I started to say that he was a rotten man and selfish, but Sammy said, "Forget it. Let's go to the next place." That's what we did, but Mr. Nettleman still bugged me.

We started to get gobs and piles of pennies in our club jar, so I decided to forget about Mr. Nettleman and keep asking everyone else. Someone gave me a bag of nickels. I asked the club if it was okay to take nickels in a penny drive, and everyone said it was great because you can buy a wheelchair with nickels or pennies. They don't care at the wheelchair store.

Aside from the money for Joseph, we were also getting ready for the field day. I was working hard on my skills, especially jumping rope, because I was the only boy doing that contest, and I wanted to win.

I got so I could jump one hundred fifty times without missing. Sometimes I lost count, and then I would waste lots of jumps trying to decide if I should keep on counting or start over or what.

I learned to throw my Frisbee flat and not slanted so it would go far and not right down into the dirt. On long jump practice day, I went first so I could go sit with William. There was something I wanted to talk with him about.

"You're still signed up for the fifty-yard dash," I said.

"Yep," said William. "I've been practicing at home."

"Are you getting faster?"

"Yep," said William. "I put on my turbochargers and *zoom!*"

I didn't say anything, because I know he didn't have turbochargers for his wheelchair. Then I started to wonder if he did have some and that would not be fair at all, because nobody would have a chance if he just blasted off for the finish line.

I said, "No fair on the turbochargers." Then I felt bad for saying it, and I didn't say it again. After a while I said, "Want me to help you practice?"

William said, "Yep, sure. Can you come over sometime? How about today?"

I said I would if my mom said it was okay.

Mom said it was a great idea, so I got to go over there after I finished my chores. I ran right over to Mrs. Peeples's house, because that was William's house too.

William's mom said to come right in. She said, "Scoot your little self right back to the backyard, Tommy. Willie's itching to get started." So I scooted myself back there.

William wheeled himself around the backyard for a while, but then I said, "This is nuts. There's not fifty yards here at all, so we can't race."

We asked if we could go to the park, so we would have a track to race on. Mrs. Peeples said okay, and I called my mom and she said okay. So William and I walked over to the park. Well, I pushed, and William rolled.

When we got to the track, I marked out about what I thought fifty yards would be. Then we lined up on the starting line and we said, "Ready, set, go!"

I started to run, and I ran and ran, but then I looked back and there was William, still just getting started. I said, "This is crazy," and I ran back and grabbed his wheelchair handles and ran as fast as I could to the finish line!

"Wow," said William. "That was fun!"

I thought it was a good thing that William wasn't allowed to have anyone push him in the race or he might win it after all.

11
Cheers for William

One day the high school boys said to sit down in a circle on the grass. Nathan said, "We're going to talk about running today."

I said, "Yea!" because I'm the running man. I was all set to race against William and win a blue ribbon.

Nathan said, "The first thing to remember in a race is not to start running until the referee says 'Go!'"

"Is someone going to shoot a gun?" Howie asked. Howie said at track meets someone is always shooting a gun instead of saying go.

I said, "Do people get shot?"

Howie said I didn't know anything at all.

Nathan said there wouldn't be any guns at all, just somebody's mom or dad saying, "Ready, set, go!"

The second thing about running fast for fifty
yards is to run as fast as you can and don't slow
down until you have already passed the finish line.

"And be sure you never look behind you."

"Why not look behind?" said Melodie. "What
if you are in first place and you want to see where
everyone else is?"

"Because sometimes when you look behind,
you might slow down, or you might trip on
something." That's what William said.

I said that William couldn't trip on anything,
but Melodie gave me a mean look that said I
should be quiet.

Then we did some races. First, five boys lined
up in a straight line. The big boys showed us on
the field how far fifty yards
was, and one of the girls
went down there to make
sure we ran far enough.

When it was my turn to run, I ran as fast as I could. I didn't look back or slow down one bit. Sammy won, but I came in second. When I finished, I looked back and there was William. He was pushing and pushing his chair. And nobody was cheering for us guys who came in ahead of him. All the girls were cheering for William!

I said, "What?"

But nobody answered me.

It took William a long time to finish the race, but finally he did and everyone cheered for him.

I said that wasn't fair, but Sammy said to forget about it. "It doesn't matter who gets *cheered* for," he said. "It matters who *wins*."

"Okay!" I said.

12
Field Day

It was field day at last! I was so excited that I
got to the park at nine o'clock in the morning even
though nothing would start until eleven. At first
no one was there at all, but then people started
to arrive and set up tables and chairs and games.
Mom came and set up her wooden clown that you
throw the beanbag through its mouth and you get a
whistle. Howie's mom and dad had a booth where
you could toss a ring around a bottle, and if you
did it you got a toy. They let me try before they
were actually open, but I missed five times!

The mayor came and talked loud into the
microphone. He said welcome to our first annual
field day, and he was sure it was going to be great.
He said to stop by the city booth, and he would
give all the kids a treat, so we went right over

there. We got to shake the mayor's hand, and he gave us candy.

Then it was time for our contests. First was Frisbee throw. William threw his Frisbee right into the ground on accident. This made him mad. I thought it would be good for me, and I threw a good throw, but my throw didn't go straight at all, but crazy sideways. It knocked Mrs. Mingo right in the stomach!

I said, "Oh no, sorry."

She said, "It's okay, don't worry about it."

Boy, oh boy, did I feel silly!

I got a white ribbon for jumping rope. Third place! I got up to a hundred and sixty-three, but Melodie jumped up to three hundred and thirty-nine! Even then she didn't miss, but just stopped. I told her good job. At first I thought I would hide my crummy white ribbon in my pocket—I wanted blue!—but then I thought that some kind of ribbon is better than no ribbon, right? So I pinned it on my shirt like everyone else was doing with their ribbons.

I tried some other games like dropping clothespins into a jar and throwing a ring around the bottles, but then I heard the loudspeaker say, "Eight-year-old boys' fifty-yard dash in five minutes!" That made me jump. It was finally time for our big race, and it was my last hope for a blue ribbon!

I ran over to the track as fast as I could. The stands were full of cheering parents. I saw my mom and dad up there. Mom waved at me, and Dad gave me a thumb's up sign that means, "You can do it!"

I saw old Mrs. Peeples with her sparkly eyes and curly white hair sitting in the front row of the bleachers. Young Mrs. Peeples was there too. She had a sign that said, "Turn on the Turbochargers, Willie!"

We had to wait a few minutes at the starting line. We admired each other's ribbons. They said "good job" to me about my ribbon, even though it was only white. Only William didn't have any ribbon at all! That made me supersad.

I looked over at both Mrs. Peepleses again. They were so happy and cheering for William even before the race started! I thought about my mom's story about her grandpa and how everyone worked hard so he could get his crutches, so he could get around. I even thought about Franklin Roosevelt and how he needed help just to get from one place to another, even though he was President of the United States!

I got a funny feeling in the middle of my stomach. I went over to the other guys, and I said, "Hey, look, you guys. Sometimes people need help, you know?"

Sammy said, "Sure."

And Zack said, "So?"

But Howie looked over at William and said, "What are you thinking, Tommy?"

I said, "We all have ribbons. William is our friend, and he doesn't have any ribbons."

"You want to walk real slow and let him win?" Sammy said. "That would look ridiculous. He would be ashamed!"

"Nope," I said. "We'll go superduper fast! All of us!"

I told them my plan, and everyone was grinning real big when we lined up at our starting places.

The man said, "Gentlemen, get on your marks," and then he said, "Get set, go!"

We stood there for a second so William could get a tiny bit out in front, and then we all ran over to his chair and pushed faster than anything! I looked quick over at the stands. Everyone was standing up and cheering for us! They were clapping and laughing and shouting, "William! William! William!"

William had his hands up in the air and he was shouting, "Whooo-eee! Whoooooo-eeeeee!"

That's how William won the fifty-yard dash for eight-year-old boys.

All the moms and teachers met us at the finish line. My mom was crying and both Mrs. Peepleses were crying too, and William was shouting, "I won! I won!"

William's mom made us get in a huddle so she
could take our picture. She shouted, "These are
the boys who made a dream come true!" Then she
snapped the picture and cried some more.

Mrs. Mingo gave William a blue ribbon. She
said second place was a tie, so we all got red
ribbons. Red was good enough for me, and my
heart inside me felt really good, like when your
dog jumps up on you and licks your face.

William screamed and laughed for a long time.
All kinds of ladies came up and hugged us. Some
even kissed us and said we were "fine young
men" and stuff like that. After a while, Sammy
said, "Let's get out of here. There's way too much
kissing!" So we went over to the refreshments, and
Howie bought us all cotton candy.

While we were eating our cotton candy, Zack
said, "Oh, look."

Mr. Nettleman was walking toward us.

"Yikes," said Howie. "Let's get out of here."

"Hide," I said, but Sammy said he'd given up
hiding ever since he got in bad trouble for hiding
from his mom instead of doing chores.

Sammy said, "He's not coming to talk to us.
He's coming to get something to eat."

But Mr. Nettleman did walk right up to us. He did! He scared me to pieces because for one thing he was really tall, and for another thing he didn't like us coming into his store to ask for pennies.

"You the boys who keep asking for pennies?" Mr. Nettleman said.

We said, "Yes." I hung my head down so I could look at the ground instead of up at him.

"And you're the same boys who pushed William Peeples over the finish line?"

We said, "Yes."

Now I realized what he was going to say. He was going to say we should never have done something like that because he would never have a successful business if he was pushing other people instead of going fast himself. He was going to tell us we were stupid not to win ourselves.

He didn't say that. He just asked us to point out our moms to him. We pointed over to where William was surrounded by a bunch of girls and some moms. He said thank you and walked over that way.

"He's going to tell our moms that we are all silly little boys," I said.

We went back to eating our cotton candy, and a lady walked up to us. She said she was Miss Young

from the *Fig Street Examiner* and could she take
our pictures. We said of course, so we trotted back
over to where William was, and we all had our
pictures taken again. Miss Young said she would
try to get the picture on the sports page for the next
day because it was so nice what we did.

We said, "Wow," because none of us had ever
been in the newspaper before.

13
Front Page

We weren't on the sports page at all. The next morning, I looked at the *Fig Street Examiner* and guess what? We were on the front page. Color picture and everything. There we all were crowded around William with all our blue and red and white ribbons, all of us smiling big.

Underneath the picture was this title:

Boys' Friendship Here and Abroad

I didn't know what that meant, but when I started reading the article, I figured it out fast.

Not content with pushing their friend to be a winner on the track, these boys of Fig Street have organized a drive to raise money for a boy in Kenya who needs a wheelchair. Donations for Pennies for Joseph can be made at a number of Main Street businesses.

*In a related development, Mr. Marvin Nettleman
of Nettleman's Medical Supply has announced that
he will donate a new wheelchair if the Pennies
for Joseph drive raises enough money to ship
the chair to Kenya. "When I saw these children
help their friend win his race," Nettleman said,
"it touched my heart. I wanted to do something. I
wanted to help out."*

I almost fell over when I read that! All I could
think about was that we didn't need four hundred
and seventy-six dollars anymore. We only needed
two hundred and twenty-nine!

Plus it turned out that when we went to collect
people's pennies that day, there were more pennies
than ever before. And on Main Street where some
businesses let us put our jars out, the jars were
full of pennies and nickels and dimes and even
quarters!

We got some coin rolls at the bank, because you
cannot just take in a wagonload of coins and say,
"Here," at the bank. You have to count it and roll
it up, and then they will give you paper money as
much as it is worth.

Nathan helped us put the coins in the wrappers
for a while, but then we got used to it. Fifty
pennies go in a penny wrapper, forty nickels to

fill a nickel paper, and fifty dimes. If you put forty quarters in a quarter wrapper, it makes ten dollars.

Finally we finished. It was time to count it all up.

We added and added and added. Twenty dollars, thirty dollars, forty dollars. Pretty soon there was over one hundred dollars!

"Keep counting!" I said. "We only need two hundred and twenty-nine dollars to ship the wheelchair!"

And so we filled penny rolls. Finally Nathan cleared his throat and said, "All right, everyone. Listen up! I have the grand total right here before me!"

We all said, "Shhh!" but the shushing was so loud, we had to say *shhh* again to get it to stop!

Then Nathan stood up and said, "I am pleased to let you know that we have a grand total of two hundred and thirty-five dollars and forty-six cents!"

We yelled! We clapped! We jumped and hugged each other.

We had done it. Joseph would get his wheelchair.

Nathan led us in a line to the bank where we traded our dollars and coins for a money order to give to the post office. Our next stop was

Nettleman's Medical Supplies. When we showed
him our money order for the shipping costs, Mr.
Nettleman smiled and said, "I knew you could
do it. You're Fig Street Kids." He walked to the
back of his store and brought out a brand-new
wheelchair. Then he let us use the phone so we
could call our moms, and all the moms came down
so we could walk to the post office together and
mail the wheelchair off to Africa.

Mr. Nettleman talked to our moms for a long

time, and I sort of listened in. He said along with
the wheelchair, he was including some medicines
that Uncle Mick's organization might need. Then
he talked to the post office man about "security

concerns" and "shipping problems." The man said
we had enough money to pay for insurance, so it
was no problem. I asked mom what all that meant,
and she said insurance was so if anything bad
happened to our shipment, the wheelchair would
be replaced for free. That made me superhappy
because what if the box never got there after all the
hard work we did? That would be the worst thing
ever!

We put other things in the box too. Pictures of
ourselves. The newspaper about our race and our
Pennies for Joseph project. And letters for Joseph.

After we paid our money and said goodbye to
our box, Mr. Nettleman said, "If the adults will
allow it, I'd like to treat all these children to ice
cream at the Triple Dip Ice Cream Shop."

The moms said yes, and we said yes too,
because ice cream is the best thing in the whole
world, especially if you just mailed a wheelchair to
Africa and you feel supergood about everything.

14
Fig Street Kids
Are Great

A few weeks went by before we got an e-mail from Kenya. Here is what the letter said:

Dear Fig Street Kids,

Thank you thank you for the wheelchair. Now I can go anywhere! I am so happy. I want to tell you thank you so much for sending the chair. Also the pictures of you. You are nice kids. The Fig Street Kids are Great!

I want to be your friend and write you more letters on the computer.

Love,

Joseph

Uncle Mick had attached a photograph. It showed him standing next to Joseph. Joseph was sitting in his wheelchair.

Joseph said we were great, and we thought we were pretty great too, but we were supertired of collecting pennies and doing extra chores, so we decided that for the rest of the summer we would just do our regular chores, like before. Our regular chores didn't seem so hard now that we had worked so hard, and we laughed about the time we tried to run away so we wouldn't have to do them at all!

William said for the rest of the summer we could meet in the clubhouse instead of in his room.

But I said, "I like your room, and I like your train."

So what happened was we traded off. The girls had the clubhouse when we went to William's room, and they met in Penny's room when we had the clubhouse. It got kind of weird in there because the girls put up pictures and brought in flowers, but we didn't mind too much because they also brought us cookies sometimes from their cooking class.

So all summer long—whether we were in William's room playing trains or sitting in my blue clubhouse eating pretzels—we would talk about going to the moon, or digging up buried treasure, how girls aren't really creepy after all, and how all of us kids on Fig Street are winners.